A New Baby Is Coming!
A Guide for a Big Brother or Sister

Written by
Emily Menendez-Aponte

Illustrated by
R. W. Alley

ONE
CARING
PLACE

Abbey Press
St. Meinrad, IN 47577

For Matthew and Sophia

Text © 2005 Emily Menendez-Aponte
Illustrations © 2005 St. Meinrad Archabbey
Published by One Caring Place
Abbey Press
St. Meinrad, Indiana 47577

Library of Congress Catalog Number
2005932493

ISBN 978-0-87029-396-2

Printed in the United States of America

A Message to Parents, Teachers, and Other Caring Adults

Expecting a new baby in the family is a very exciting and wonderful time. For a young child in the family, however, this time can also bring with it uncertainty and anxiety. Adults need to recognize the uneasiness a child may be feeling and help him or her continue to feel secure and loved.

Most young children do not have an accurate perception of time. The concept of eight or nine months is very abstract and difficult for them to understand. Try explaining the timing in terms a child can better understand. For example, the baby will be here when it is spring and warm outside again, when school is out for the summer, or when it is Christmastime.

Many things need to change when a family is preparing for a new baby. Therefore, it is important not to make other significant changes in the older brother or sister's life that could wait until another time. For example, try not to change the child's bedroom or get a new bed too close to the arrival of the baby. Continuing as many of the same routines and practices—even simple ones—can ease the arrival of the new sibling.

Children will feel more connected to the arrival of a new sibling if their family talks about the new baby in terms of "our baby," rather than Mom using the term "my baby." This simple adjustment of vocabulary can make an older child feel more accepting and welcoming of the arrival of a new sibling. Additionally, children can prepare for their new sibling by understanding that they were once babies, themselves. Get out the photo album and show them baby pictures of themselves. Talk about your preparations, excitement, and joy at that time.

Adding a new child to a family is bound to be somewhat stressful for all of the family members. But having a sibling can also be a wonderful, lifelong, enriching experience for a child. As adults, we can help children through this transition and enable them to see and experience the great joys of sharing family life with a little brother or sister.

—*Emily Menendez-Aponte*

There Is Going to Be a New Baby

There is going to be a new baby in your family! Everyone in your family is so excited and happy. Lots of people are talking about the new baby coming.

You are going to be a big brother or a big sister and you may be wondering exactly what that means. You may be a little worried about how things might change around your house.

How Do You Get a New Baby?

New babies come a couple of different ways. Sometimes, a baby will grow in your mom's tummy. Other times, babies are born somewhere else and your family adopts them.

If the baby is in your mom's tummy, her belly will get big while the baby is growing. She may feel sick or tired. But you don't have to worry— sometimes moms feel like that when they are pregnant, and your mom will be okay.

You might be able to feel the baby moving around inside your mom's tummy when you put your hands on her belly. And, even though the baby can't see you yet, he can hear you. Ask your mom if you can feel her belly or talk to the baby.

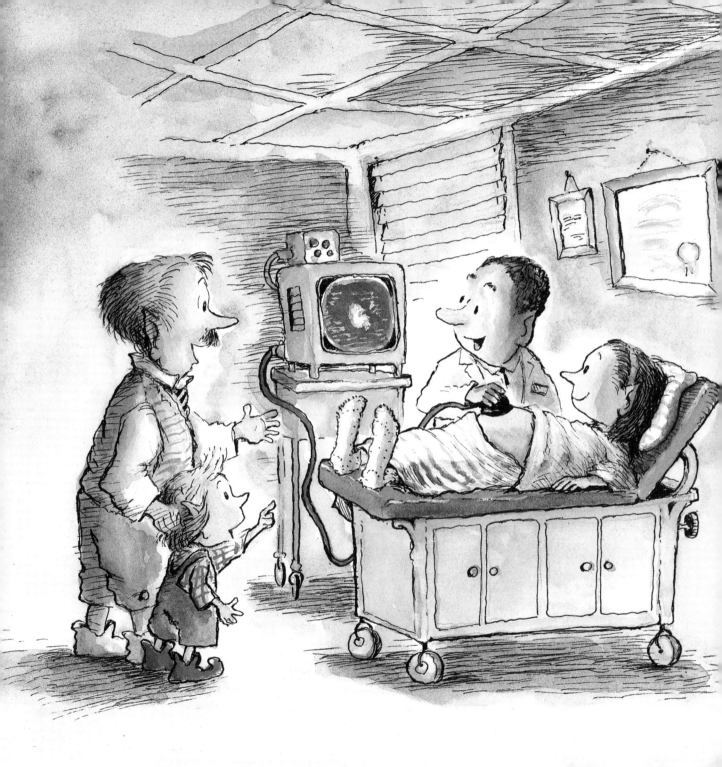

It's a Long Time to Wait

It can feel like a long time to wait until the new baby is born. It takes a while for the baby to grow big enough until it is ready to come out. Ask your mom and dad when the baby will be coming.

Your family will probably do things to get ready for the new baby. They may paint and decorate a room in your house. They might buy new things, or use things from when you were a baby.

You may feel a little upset that a new baby is going to be using your things. Talk to your mom and dad if you feel upset. Maybe they have saved one special thing that no one else gets to use.

You Were a Baby Once, Too

Did you know you were a baby once, too? You were a tiny little baby and your parents did all of the same kinds of things to get ready for you.

They were so excited when they knew you were going to be born. They probably got a room ready for you, and bought new things for you. They even talked about what to name you. They did all of the same things to get ready for you that they are doing now to get ready for the new baby.

You can ask your mom and dad about what it was like when you were a baby and maybe look at some pictures, too.

When the Baby Is Born

Soon it will be time for the baby to be born. Your parents may go to a hospital, where a doctor will help the baby come out of your mom's belly. Or, your parents may have to travel somewhere to adopt your new little brother or sister. Either way, soon they will come home and bring your new brother or sister with them.

You will probably go to your grandma's house or someone will come to stay at your house while your parents are gone. You might miss your mom and dad while they are gone, and they will miss you, too. You will be able to talk to them on the phone and maybe even visit the hospital. Whoever is taking care of you will do all the same things your mom and dad usually do and probably some extra fun things.

Some Things Change...
Some Things Stay the Same

When a new baby comes into your family, lots of things will change, but lots of things will stay the same.

Your house may seem a little busier and there may be lots of new "baby stuff" around. But all of your things will still be there, too. You will still have your favorite teddy bear and all your same toys. You will still go to school and get to play with your friends.

You can talk to your mom and dad about anything you are worried about that might change or not be the same.

What Will the Baby Do?

New babies aren't able to do very much at first. Usually, babies sleep a lot, eat a lot, and cry a lot. Babies can do hardly anything for themselves. Your mom and dad will spend a lot of time taking care of the new baby.

Sometimes, it's no fun to have a baby who can't play with you and spends so much time sleeping. But soon the baby will get bigger and be able to do more fun things besides sleep, eat, and cry.

Mommy and Daddy Are Busy

Because babies can't do anything on their own like you can, it may seem like Mom or Dad is always busy with the baby. It can be really hard to hear your mom say, "You have to wait a minute."

Babies do take a lot of time, but your mom and dad will give you some special time, too. If you are feeling left out, ask your mom or dad to play a game with you or read you a story. Just remember that sometimes you will have to be patient.

Does Mommy Still Love Me?

When a new baby comes into your family, you may wonder if your mom and dad still love you. Or if they will love the new baby more than you.

Your mom and dad will still love you just as much after the baby comes as they did before. They love you very, very much and always will—no matter what.

It can be hard to share your parents with a new brother or sister; but your parents will love you both just the same. They won't love one more than the other. New babies just make your mom and dad grow more love!

Feeling Grumpy and Mad

You might get a little grumpy or even feel mad at the new baby. That's okay. Everybody gets a little grumpy and mad sometimes.

You might even say, "I hate the baby." It is hard when so many things change and your mommy and daddy have to spend so much time taking care of the baby.

When you feel angry or upset, tell your mom or dad. Maybe you can play with a special toy that is just for you. Maybe your mom can spend some special time with you.

Being a Helper

When you become a big brother or big sister, you will probably get to do things to help. You might be able to help your mom hold the baby, or help feed the baby. You may be able to help by going to get a diaper or a toy for the baby.

You can also help teach the baby new things like smiling and laughing and making funny noises. But you always have to remember to ask your mom or dad first.

Lots of Visitors

When a new baby is born, lots of people want to come and visit. New babies are cute and fun to look at. People like to see them and hold them when they are first born.

Friends and people in your family will come to your house to visit the baby.

The visitors will probably bring presents for the baby and maybe even some little ones for you, too. When people come to visit, ask if you can show the baby to them. You can say, "Hi Grandma, this is my new baby sister."

The Baby Will Get Older

Soon, the baby will grow and not even be a baby anymore. The baby will be able to do some things for herself, just like you. Your mom and dad won't have to do everything. She won't cry as much, and won't have to be held as often.

When the baby gets older, you will be able to play together and laugh and be silly together. Your new brother or sister will be able to walk and run with you and will even be able to talk to you. You will have a chance to teach her all kinds of new things—like your favorite game. You will have lots of fun together.

A New Family

Having a new baby join your family can be really hard, but can be lots of fun. Things will change some in your house, and your mom and dad will be really busy. But not all changes are bad.

You will still have lots of love and special times with your mom and dad. You will also now have lots of fun with your new brother or sister.

Best of all, you will have lots of special times together as a family.

Emily Menendez-Aponte holds a B.A. in Psychology and a Master of Social Work degree. As a licensed social worker, she has counseled families and children for over 10 years. Currently, she lives in New Jersey with her husband and two children and is an independent consultant for the New Jersey Early Intervention System.

R. W. Alley is the illustrator for the popular Abbey Press adult series of Elf-help books, as well as an illustrator and writer of children's books. He lives in Barrington, Rhode Island, with his wife, daughter, and son. See a wide variety of his works at: www.rwalley.com.